Until We Meet Again, Leo

A CHILDREN'S BOOK ON NAVIGATING LOSS

Written by Alexandra McGroarty
Illustrated by Jenna Gelow

atmosphere press

Published by Atmosphere Press

atmospherepress.com

To Lucas and Ava

The steaming tropical jungles of India are home to a billion animals. Nature sings a billion magical songs here. Every animal is remembered with great love and respect. Their songs go on forever.

The god of all Indian animals was golden Pashupati. Pashupati decided the ruler of each species, and was especially proud of making Gajaraj the king of the elephants. Gajaraj ruled for many years with strength, wisdom, bravery and kindness. The elephants loved him. When the great Gajaraj died, the elephants mourned for him, but also celebrated his goodness and his life.

In the great temple Hathi Paga Majal, which means "elephant leg palace," the elephants built a gigantic, magnificent statue of Gajaraj. Each day flowers were brought, until the statue itself was covered with brilliant petals in a hundred colors.

"It's even more beautiful this way," the elephants agreed.

Whenever the elephants missed Gajaraj's wisdom or leadership, they thought, "What would Gajaraj have us do?" The elephants remembered their king so well that they always knew what to do. Time passed, and Pashupati saw that the elephants needed no new ruler at all. Their memory of Gajaraj was enough.

In the Elephant Kingdom, the mighty Kaveri River thundered through the jungle, bringing water to all the animals. The Kaveri River was strong and violent, sometimes bringing too much water, ruining food and homes. A giant dam held the Kaveri River so just the right amount of water came through the jungle.

But one year, the rain was so intense and the water rose so high that the dam began to creak and crumble. The elephant tribe hurried to see what they could do.

Among the elephants, brave young Leo faced the mighty Kaveri River, with his best friend Veda beside him.

Veda told Leo, “If the dam breaks, a million acres of food will be lost, and many animals could drown!”

Suddenly the wild Kaveri River broke through the dam, unleashing a terrifying wave of water.

Veda cried, “Run, Leo, before the waters take us under!”

Instead of running, however, Leo charged into the water's path. He planted his thick elephant feet into the ground and planted his broad elephant head against the dam wall. Grunting and straining with all his might, he shoved the river back, back, back.

He feared at any moment the water might be stronger than him. But then he thought of the other jungle animals who might suffer if the river got away, and he pushed harder than ever, until he held the broken dam in place.

Veda trumpeted with joy. “Quickly, everyone! While Leo holds the dam, bring logs to strengthen it!”

The elephants rushed into the jungle, using their trunks to pull trees from the ground and haul them to the dam. Each tree they brought made the dam thicker and sturdier.

They worked for three days and nights to save the jungle. Leo kept his head pushed hard and his feet planted firm.

Each time he felt tired, Veda was there to say, “Hold on, Leo! You can do it!”

Hearing her, he felt stronger.

On the third day, Veda reported, “The work is almost done! But there is so much water still. I’m worried it might top over the dam, even after all our work!”

Leo told her, “You will surely think of something.”

“Thank you, Leo. Hey, I know! We must make a path for the water, so it can escape without hurting anything.”

Veda bounded away, and directed the elephants to dig a deep channel with their tusks, so all the extra water had a place to go.

On the fourth day, Veda did not stop to talk as she had before. Though he missed her, Leo knew that their combined work would save the jungle. He looked forward to resting and celebrating with Veda and all the elephants who worked so hard.

When he finally stepped away from the repaired dam, Leo turned to see the elephant tribe behind him, their heads hanging in sadness. Their distress confused him.

“What is wrong?” asked Leo. “We have repaired the dam!”

The oldest elephant in the tribe, Sanjay, stepped forward. “Yes, Leo. We will always remember that you held the dam four entire days while we worked. But, I have some terrible news. As we finished the channel, the river’s heavy water came roaring through. Thank goodness the channel worked exactly as Veda hoped it would... but Veda was caught in the rushing waters.”

“But where is she? Is she all right now?” demanded Leo.

“No, Leo. We’re so sorry. Veda was swept underneath, and she died.”

The elephants built a statue of Veda made from shining black stone, right next to the flower-covered statue of Gajaraj in the Hathi Paga Majal. On the pedestal her name was written, “Veda the Wise,” and the story of how she devised the plan to channel the Kaveri River.

Veda's body was washed and wrapped in a clean white cloth. Leo thought she looked asleep. But if she were just sleeping, she could dream, and rest, and wake up again. This was not sleeping. This was just Veda's body, but her spirit, the thing that made her a wise and funny best friend to Leo, was no longer inside.

"If she's not in her body, where is she?" Leo asked Sanjay.

"There are many beliefs about where our spirits might go," said Sanjay.

Frustrated, Leo asked elephant after elephant where they believed spirits might go. The more answers he got, the more confused he became. Some said Veda would return to earth as a new animal, some said she would go to paradise, some said she would remain in peaceful quiet forever, and some said that she would journey to an amazing afterlife. No one knew for certain.

There was a beautiful funeral ceremony with candles and incense. While all these things happened, Leo felt worse and worse. The only thing he wanted to do was talk to Veda about how bad he felt – yet Veda was dead.

Sanjay told Leo that the ceremony would help them say goodbye to Veda.

“I don’t want to say goodbye to her. I want her back,” Leo insisted.

Sanjay understood, and tried to explain. “Losing an elephant we love is very difficult. With time, it will not hurt so badly or feel so frightening.”

“No!” shouted Leo, startling every elephant around. “This is wrong! Veda and I saved the jungle from the Kaveri River. It isn’t fair that Veda is dead. I demand that she be returned! Pashupati must give her back!”

How could Leo make his demand to Pashupati? He thought hard. All animal rulers were selected by Pashupati, so they all must know the golden god. But right now, there was no elephant king to ask.

“Never mind,” said Leo. “There are a billion animals in the jungle, and each species has a ruler. I will find one who will make Pashupati give Veda back to us.”

Leo left his home, telling no one where he was going. He walked slowly and sadly across Kerala, the southernmost point of beautiful India. When he saw other elephant tribes, they recognized him and called out, thanking him for saving the jungle. He raised his trunk, but was too sad to stop and talk. His massive legs felt almost too weary to carry him.

The Elephant Kingdom was vast, because elephants are the largest animals on land. It took ever so long to find the end of elephant lands, moving finally north into Karnataka.

This was the cows' country. Leo followed the roads to the palace of Sindhi Kama, their Queen. She had soft brown eyes with long lashes, and shining white horns. A purple robe wrapped around her thick, strong neck. Something in her face showed that she understood his sadness.

“Hero of the elephants, welcome,” greeted the kind Sindhi Kama.

“Greetings, Sindhi Kama.” Leo bowed. “I need your help to speak to Pashupati, God of the Animals, so he can give back my friend Veda.”

Sindhi Kama shook her head. “Pashupati does not return the dead to us. Death and life are partners in the world.”

That was not what Leo wanted to hear. “If death and life are partners, then why does this hurt me so much?”

Sindhi Kama did not mind Leo’s temper. “Because you miss your friend—you are sad. Cows understand sadness very well. When someone we love dies, we feel many things. Some, like sadness, are painful. Sadness may always stay with us, but it can combine with other feelings to become wisdom, respect, and thankfulness. You will see.”

“No I won’t! I hate being sad! I’m so angry I want to stomp the jungle to the ground!” Leo stomped then, jarring the walls of the Cows’ palace. “I’m angry at death and angry at Pashupati and angry at Veda too!”

“Anger is another feeling death brings.” Sindhi Kama produced a map, and planted her hoof on it to show Leo where to go. “Keep traveling north, to the temple of Bengal Chitan, King of the Tigers. He is extremely wise about anger.”

Leo was almost too big to fit into the dense forests of Maharashtra, but in the thick trees Leo found an ancient, shaded temple. Bengal Chitan, a huge tiger, had black stripes as dark as night, and orange stripes bright as sunshine. He dozed atop his temple, draped in golden silk.

The trees shook as Leo stomped near. The King of Tigers yawned, irritated by Leo's loud interruption. His grumbling tiger subjects leapt higher into the trees. Bengal Chitan announced, "You're a long way from home, noisy Elephant."

Leo explained his need to speak to Pashupati, to bring Veda back. "That is why I'm so angry. I'm even angry at Veda! None of this is fair!"

Bengal Chitan agreed. "It does seem unfair. We tigers get quite angry about death. Nothing wrong with anger—so long as we don't bite each other."

"But what do I do?"

"Sharpen your claws on a tree, then have a good nap," suggested Bengal Chitan. Then he examined Leo and saw that he had no claws. "Oh – well, perhaps you tell your other elephant friends about it. Cats aren't big talkers, but it can help."

"Can't Pashupati just give Veda back?"

"Pashupati clearly likes tigers best of any animal, but I would not ask him for such a favor. Pashupati does not return the dead to us."

"What!" Leo exclaimed in horror. "You won't help me either? Won't anyone understand? It's my fault that Veda died – I have to do something!"

"Your fault!" Bengal Chitan looked surprised. "That is guilt. Oh, we tigers know nothing of guilt, for everything we do is perfection." He curled his tail to point northward. "Follow the Narmada River, to the land of the monkey tribes. Speak to Monkey King Gray Verana. He knows more of guilt than anyone."

Leo moved north on the shores of the Narmada River into the lands of Madhya Pradesh. The path became a dirt road that divided the wilderness from a secluded human village on the plains.

Suddenly Leo saw a hundred monkeys dash outside the village gates, laughing wildly as they tumbled toward the jungle. Gray Verana was the last one out of the village, his blue silk jacket flapping in the wind. The Monkey King caught sight of Leo and leapt onto his back in three easy jumps. Several other monkeys joined him.

"Just in time!" Gray Verana said to Leo. "Now run for it!"

Startled, Leo ran down the road with King Gray Verana. Five – then ten – then twenty more monkeys leapt on his back! Leo turned his head to see humans rushing out from the town, yelling after them. Some of these humans had funny mustaches painted on their faces, some were missing their shoes.

As he charged ahead, Leo asked, "What happened?"

"We just did every prank in the book." Verana showed Leo a book which, indeed, was called *Monkey Pranks.* "Better hurry! Faster, faster!"

The humans gave up the chase, and the monkeys dispersed. Leo continued to trot along the road while only King Gray Verana lazily rested on his back. "Ah, this is the best way to travel," said the Monkey King.

Leo's mood grew dark again. "I shouldn't be laughing," he said. "It's not right to laugh and have fun if my friend Veda has died."

"Why, that's not true at all," said Gray Verana. "Veda would want those things for such a good friend as you."

"You don't understand. Veda died in the Kaveri River flood. If I had worked harder and faster, I could have saved her. It's all my fault. I was a very bad friend."

Gray Verana made Leo stop. He swung around and sat on Leo's trunk, so they could see eye-to-eye. The Monkey King said, "You feel guilty. I suppose that cranky tiger told you to ask me about guilt, right? But your problem is different, poor elephant."

"You must ask Pashupati to bring Veda back," said Leo. "I didn't mean for her to die."

Gently, Gray Verana patted Leo's forehead. "When we lose someone we love, most of us do feel guilty. We imagine that we did something bad, or made a mistake. We think of things we could have done differently. But our thoughts and actions do not make death happen. If you told your friend about your guilty feelings, what would she say?"

"Oh!" exclaimed Leo. "Veda would say that I did my best, and nothing that happened was my fault."

“Veda sounds very wise. All we can ever do is try our best, and keep learning if we make mistakes. But I cannot ask Pashupati to bring her back, my friend.”

Leo wanted to argue, but he was all out of ideas. “What can I do? I still feel sad, and angry, and guilty too.”

“Yes, I know. I have lost someone before, and I felt sad, and angry, and guilty. This went on for some time. Ah – time is the problem!” Gray Verana jumped off Leo’s trunk. “You must travel to the hills outside the great city of Delhi. Speak with Queen Cobra Sheesha. She is the expert on time.”

Leo never realized how big India was until he walked all the way to Delhi, its biggest and busiest city. He did not approach, but stood at midnight on a high hill in the distance, gazing down at the million homes shining with lamplight. “I wish that Veda could see how beautiful this is,” said Leo.

“You must enjoy its beauty for her,” said a slithery, motherly voice from behind him. “It is kind of you to share this beauty with the memory of your friend.”

Leo turned to see Queen Cobra Sheesha on a rock. She was a thick, black snake with golden eyes and a dramatic hood. A silky white cloth draped around her smooth black scales. The enormous full moon in the night sky shone down on her, as well as the glow of the city in the distance.

"I have walked a million miles," Leo told Sheesha, "but no animal rulers think Pashupati will let Veda come back. I guess you'll tell me the same thing."

"It is true," said Queen Cobra Sheesha. "Pashupati does not undo death."

"Then this whole trip has been a waste of time."

"Ah, time is my expertise," said the queen. Her tongue flicked in the air as she thought. "Time is never wasted. Have you learned nothing?"

Leo shrugged his elephant shoulders. "Lots of animals understand what it's like when someone dies. The feelings hurt, but they are important, and it's okay to have them. But, please tell me that soon, all these bad feelings will go away forever!"

Queen Cobra Sheesha let out a long, hissing sigh. "I cannot tell you that. You loved Veda so much that I think in your heart you will always feel some sadness, some anger, maybe even some guilt. Just remember, these feelings change, grow, and make new feelings. Thankfulness. Happiness. Courage. Change and growth take time, Leo. Give yourself time."

"How much?" asked Leo.

"All of it," said Queen Cobra Sheesha, swishing quietly away. "Take all the time you need. Good journey, Leo..."

Leo walked south for countless days until he saw the familiar kingdom of the Elephants once more. When at last he arrived at the Hathi Paga Majal, night had fallen. Everyone was asleep.

Though his elephant feet ached from the journey, Leo still went to the monuments. Veda's black stone elephant stood next to the flower-covered Gajaraj. Leo put his trunk on Veda's stone statue's head. Speaking to her statue, he told her about his long trip and the animals he had met.

When he finished, he said, "Oh Veda, I miss you so much."

Then he began to cry. He cried and cried and cried some more. He didn't want to stop.

"Veda was a great elephant," said a voice next to Leo.

A bit startled, Leo looked up to see... Pashupati! The God of Animals stood before him, tall as Leo, with golden skin and four arms!

Leo stumbled back, almost too surprised to speak. But he did not forget his important wish. "I want Veda back. Please. All the animals say you won't do it! Why won't you?"

Pashupati's face was kind. "I wish I could. If I could bring back great elephants, Gajaraj himself would still be alive. But death cannot be undone, not even by me. Death is part of the cycle that rules us all."

Leo began crying again. "Can you at least make it stop hurting?"

"Hurting for Veda is a part of loving her."

Pashupati shook his great head. "Come and look at this."

He took Leo to the foot of the great statue of Gajaraj, and began pushing flowers aside. Beneath many soft, fragrant orange petals there was a stone with words on it – very much like the stone that told of Veda's heroism. This one, beneath Gajaraj, contained a simple poem.

Although you may miss me, I'm with you each day,
For we are connected in every way.
No, nothing that's living can always stay here.
Each one of us has an adventure to play.

And as I depart on the biggest dream yet,
please think of me dearly and have no regret.
For when you remember, I am always near.
We all know that elephants never forget.

Pashupati wiped a tear away as he said, "The elephants remember Gajaraj with so much love. And you will remember Veda. She died, a very hard thing for you to endure. But she will never be gone, Leo. She is part of you."

Was that true? Leo closed his eyes and thought hard, and realized that Pashupati was right. He felt Veda there inside him. He could imagine her voice saying, "Hold on, Leo. You can do it!" And hearing her, he felt stronger.

When Leo opened his eyes, Pashupati had vanished once more.

Tired from his long journey, Leo thought it might be nice to lie down next to Veda's statue and have a good sleep full of dreams.

In the morning, he would tell the other elephants about the amazing things he had seen and learned, and all the feelings that were okay to feel, even if they hurt. He would tell them all about searching for Veda, only to find her right there inside his heart.

About the Author

Alexandra founded McGroarty & Co. Consulting and serves as the lead Human Resources consultant. Alex is a certified Diversity Professional as well as a Certified Professional Coach. She recently obtained a Graduate Certificate from Cornell University in Sustainability.

Alexandra lives with her two children, Lucas and Ava, their two dogs, Sugar and Fiona, and a cat named Scrambles, in New Jersey. In her free time, she likes to spend time with family, travel, and volunteer in the Greater Philadelphia area.

About the Illustrator

With a background in graphic design, Jenna runs Jenna Gelow Designs, covering all things: social media, logo design, web design, digital marketing and branding. Jenna was born and raised in South Jersey and attended the Art Institute of Philadelphia, and over the last 12 years she has continued to build her portfolio working with various small businesses. In her free time, she enjoys crafting custom wood pieces and signs, spending time with friends and family, and most importantly her pup, Kodi.

About Atmosphere Press

Atmosphere Press is an independent, full-service publisher for excellent books in all genres and for all audiences. Learn more about what we do at atmospherepress.com.

We encourage you to check out some of Atmosphere's latest releases, which are available at Amazon.com and via order from your local bookstore:

Alley: I Have Albinism, by Alethea Allen
Santa on a Surfboard, by Laura Sharp
Lilah Loves Life, by Brian Sullivan
The Christmas Witch, by Jaime Katusha
My Sister is Sick… What About Me?, by Mary Kay and Eli Olson
There's a Spider in My Bed, by Devon Nunnally and Biaina Alexanian
Yikes, I Saw a Barracuda!, by Tamara Anderson
Winston's Big Wind, by Barbara Reyelts
Finnigan the Finicky Donkey, by Ashley Vail
Holidays in Trees: Harvest Festival, by Cammy Marble
I Have Worry Monsters in My Tummy, by Erica Wilson, M.ED., LPC., NCC
The Tail of a Trio, by Katherine Scott
Cow Days, by Christina Warfel
Logan and Lexi Meditate, by Denesia D. Rogers
It's Just a Heart, by Kathy Kay

Ingram Content Group UK Ltd.
Milton Keynes UK
UKHW051158110723
424889UK00004B/32